FURRY AND FLO

capstone
young readers

Furry and Flo is published by
Capstone Young Readers
A Capstone Imprint
1710 Roe Crest Drive
North Mankato, MN 56003
www.capstoneyoungreaders.com

Library of Congress Cataloging-in-Publication Data
Troupe, Thomas Kingsley, author.
The solemn golem / by Thomas Kingsley Troupe ; illustrated by Stephen Gilpin.

pages cm. -- (Furry and Flo)

Summary: A sad golem has come through the portal, and after hearing his story, Flo and
Furry return with him to Furry's world to help him defeat the cruel golem master who
made him — and end up trapped in the other world when the portal is damaged.

ISBN 978-1-4342-9646-7 (library binding) -- ISBN 978-1-62370-172-7 (paper over
board) -- ISBN 978-1-4965-0175-2 (eBook PDF)

1. Werewolves--Juvenile fiction. 2. Golem--Juvenile fiction. 3. Monsters--Juvenile fiction.
4. Best friends--Juvenile fiction. [1. Werewolves--Fiction. 2. Golem--Fiction. 3. Monsters-
-Fiction. 4. Best friends--Fiction. 5. Friendship--Fiction.] I. Gilpin, Stephen, illustrator. II.
Title.

PZ7.T7538So 2015

813.6--dc23

2014027309

Artistic effects: Shutterstock/Kataleks Studio (background)

Book design by Hilary Wacholz

Printed in China.
092014
008472RRDS15

SOLEMN GOLEM

BOOK 6

BY THOMAS KINGSLEY TROUPE
ILLUSTRATED BY STEPHEN GILPIN

TABLE OF

CHAPTER 1
WHOLE LOT OF SHAKING..6

CHAPTER 2
WRECKING BALL..16

CHAPTER 3
GARVEL THE MISERABLE...24

CHAPTER 4
NUMBER 19...34

CHAPTER 5
RUBBLE SMUGGLE..46

CHAPTER 6
THE HILLS ARE ALIVE...58

CONTENTS

CHAPTER 7
NOT A NICE GUY...70

CHAPTER 8
TWENTY IS PLENTY...82

CHAPTER 9
GRAVEYARD...94

CHAPTER 10
GOLEM GORGE...104

CHAPTER 11
THE PROBLEM WITH PORTALS..114

WHOLE LOT OF SHAKING

CHAPTER 1

Flo Gardner wasn't *normally* the kind of girl who had nightmares . . . but her life lately was far from normal. Ever since she and her mother had moved to Corman Towers, a run-down apartment building in the middle of the city, things had been strange to say the least.

Corman Towers wasn't like other apartment buildings. Down in the basement laundry room, hidden behind the dryers,

was a glowing blue crack in the floor. Flo had quickly learned that the crack was much more than just a flaw in the cement. It was a portal to another world — a world filled with all sorts of monsters.

But not everything that came through the crack was bad news. In fact, that's how Flo's best friend, Ferdinand Babbitt, better known as Furry, had ended up in her world. Just like Corman Towers wasn't exactly a regular apartment building, Furry wasn't exactly a regular third-grade boy. He was actually a werewolf who had escaped the monster world to come live in Flo's.

As long as Furry and the portal shard he'd stolen from his werewolf father stayed in the human world, the portal could never be fully sealed. Every so often, creatures slipped through the crack and into Corman Towers. Some appeared by accident, and some came over for the sole purpose of finding Furry and bringing him back where he belonged. Giant spiders, goblins, mummies, skeletons . . . Furry and Flo had battled them all. But it was their most recent opponent that was giving Flo nightmares.

In Flo's dream, she was running down the hallway of Raimi Elementary School. The building was quiet and empty, and the only sounds she heard were her own footsteps slapping against the tile floors.

Flo reached the door to her fourth-grade classroom and tugged — locked. As she glanced up through the glass panel in the door, a pale face appeared on the other side — Vane, the vampire bounty hunter.

Flo jerked away from the door and took off down the hallway. She looked to her left and right at the classrooms she passed. In each doorway, she saw the silent hunter, watching her. As she reached the end of the hall, mist swirled up from an empty mason jar sitting on the floor. In seconds, Vane had materialized. Before Flo could scream, he leaped at her, and the entire school began to shake, rumbling the ground beneath her feet.

* * *

"No!" Flo cried, sitting up in bed and gasping for air. She opened her eyes and looked around. Her room was filled with the bright Sunday morning sunshine, and she was surrounded by all her favorite things: comic books, hooded sweatshirts, and her Dyno-Katz lunchbox. Vane was nowhere to be seen.

Except for the math test she needed to study for, there was nothing to worry about.

Good, Flo thought. *I've had enough excitement for a while.*

She hopped out of bed, setting her bare feet on the worn carpet in her bedroom. As she did, the floor beneath her rumbled ever so slightly, just as it had in her nightmare.

"That's not good," Flo said. It almost felt like an earthquake, but that sort of thing didn't usually happen where they lived.

Flo went out into the living room and found her mom sitting on the couch folding laundry and watching a cheesy-looking game show. On the TV screen, a guy with a giant mustache jumped up and down with excitement as he guessed the correct price of a can of peas.

"Hey, Mom," Flo said. "Did you feel that?"

"Feel what?" Mom asked, looking up. "Good morning, by the way."

"Good morning," Flo said quickly. "The floor was rumbling. I hope no one's taking a wrecking ball to this place."

Mom shook her head. "This place isn't *that* bad, Flo," she said with a little laugh. "It was probably just the boys downstairs. Besides, I'm sure Mr. Rockford would let us know if they planned to knock down Corman Towers." She winked at Flo.

"Curtis *used* to be the caretaker here, Mom," Flo said. "He's retired, so I don't think he'd know any sooner than we would. And for the record, I do like living here."

But whether she liked Corman Towers or not, Flo was still worried about the rumbling floor. It sure hadn't felt like the rambunctious Peterson brothers wrestling in the apartment below.

Maybe Furry knows what's going on, Flo thought. She hurried back to her bedroom to get changed. If the rumbling she'd felt was related to the basement crack — which it likely was — she didn't want to deal with

13

whatever had come though while wearing her pajamas.

Once Flo was dressed, she quickly ate a bowl of cereal and restocked her lunchbox with four sandwiches, two grape-flavored juice pouches, and two bags of Chee-Zee Chips. It never hurt to be prepared.

"I'm going to see what Furry's up to, Mom!" Flo shouted, heading for the front door. She opened it and stepped into the hallway. "Maybe hit the park."

Flo turned around and almost jumped out of her skin when she saw Furry standing right in front of her. He was barefoot and wore nothing more than his beat-up pair of swimming trunks.

"Jeez!" Flo said. "Don't sneak up on me like that!"

"Sorry, Flo," Furry said. He peered nervously over her shoulder, like he needed to tell her something he didn't want anyone else to overhear.

Flo could guess what that look meant. "Trouble again?" she asked.

"Yep," Furry replied.

Flo sighed. "Why am I not surprised?"

WRECKING
BALL

CHAPTER 2

"So you felt the rumbling too?" Flo asked her best friend as they walked down the hallway on the seventeenth floor.

"Yeah," Furry said. He pressed the button for the elevator. "I heard some weird things too. We should check the crack — I think we've got another visitor."

"What could be big enough to make the whole building rumble?" Flo asked.

"I'm not sure," Furry replied. "But it's up to us to find out."

Flo thought back on what had escaped the portal crack so far: a giant spider, a handful of goblins, a mummy, an army of skeletons, and a vampire. Although the big mama spider had managed to beat up Corman Towers a bit, no one had been able feel it all the way up on the seventeenth floor.

Which means that whatever is down there must be enormous, she realized.

The elevator clunked and shuddered as it reached their floor. The doors slowly squeaked open. Furry and Flo stepped inside and pressed the B button to take them down to the basement.

"I had a nightmare about Vane again," Flo admitted as the elevator car started to move.

"Really?" Furry asked. "That was more than a week ago. I don't think he's coming back. He's probably still stuck inside that glass jar you trapped him in."

"Yeah, I know," Flo said. "But he was at my school in my dream."

"Was the sun out in your dream?" Furry asked.

Flo tried to remember. Even though the school was dim, she remembered seeing light shining in through the windows. "I guess so," she said. "Why?"

"Then your nightmare got it wrong," Furry said. "If it were real, Vane would've turned to dust. Sunlight and vampires don't mix, remember?"

Flo smiled. Her little friend always had a way of making her feel better. She didn't care if monsters came through the portal — she liked Furry in her world.

* * *

Moments later, Furry and Flo stood in front of the laundry room door, their mouths hanging open in shock. The doorway was wrecked, as if something gigantic had forced its way out of the room. The heavy door hung by a hinge, its metal  frame buckled and bent. The surrounding wall had cracked and crumbled.

"Holy socks," Flo whispered. Whatever had escaped from the laundry room was clearly big — and *strong*. "What could do this?"

Furry sniffed the air and studied the ground. "I don't recognize the smell," he admitted. "This will sound weird, but it's not like anything that's come through the crack before. Whatever it is, it's not alive."

Flo groaned. "Seriously? Another dead thing? Vampires, skeletons, and mummies weren't enough?"

Flo looked down and saw bits of rock and gravel on the ground. She thought they were probably from the smashed-up doorway, but wasn't sure. Through the doorway, she saw two of the dryers were knocked from their spots in front of the crack.

"Looks like Mr. Panji will have to come fix the dryers again," Flo said quietly. She remembered the last time she'd seen the appliance repairman. Furry had been chasing him through the park and away from an army of skeletons.

Good times, Flo thought.

The two friends stood quietly for a few minutes, and all Flo could think was how hard it would be to hide the crack now that the dryers were moved. She was about to say just that when she heard something. It sounded like . . .

"Someone is crying," Furry said. Flo knew his werewolf ears had probably heard the sound much sooner than she had. "Out in the back alley."

Furry led Flo into an area she'd never noticed before. It looked like a garage. Curtis's beat-up yellow pickup truck was parked inside. At the far end of the space, a hinged garage door was torn open, as if whatever had rampaged through the laundry room had also wrecked the big door to get out.

"Wow," Furry said. "This thing is trashing the place."

Curtis's truck seemed okay, although it was a little hard to tell given how beat up it already was. As they walked farther into the garage, the sound of crying seemed louder.

"Outside," Furry said.

They slipped out through the giant hole in the garage door and into the alleyway behind the building. The smell of garbage and exhaust hit Flo's nose. She covered her nose and mouth against the odor and turned around, gasping at what she saw.

Something was sitting on an old, rusty dumpster.

Something *big*.

GARVEL THE MISERABLE

CHAPTER 3

A giant creature, made entirely from large brown rocks, sat on the edge of the dumpster. It was unlike anything Flo had ever seen. It had giant blocks of stone for feet with three toes chiseled on each one. The creature's legs were as thick as barrels.

Though Flo couldn't see all of it, the creature's torso was enormous, with muscles sculpted right into the rock. Its shoulders and arms looked like huge boulders, and Flo realized that he could probably crush them in a single stomp.

But the creature's actions were at odds with its fierce appearance. It had its face buried in its hands, and it shuddered as it wept. With every sob, Flo heard the metal dumpster groan beneath his weight.

"What is that?" Flo whispered.

Furry was silent, and Flo could tell just by looking at him that his werewolf senses were going crazy. His nose was twitching, and he was focused straight ahead. It was always funny to see him act like a dog while in his human form. Flo was just thankful that Furry didn't pee on the fire hydrants they passed whenever they went to the park.

"I think," Furry began, taking a cautious step forward, "this is a golem."

"A what now?" Flo said.

"A golem," Furry repeated. "It's like a monster built out of stuff and brought to life. I've heard of these. They can be made out of pretty much anything. This one looks like it's made of stone."

Flo watched the golem carefully. Furry's explanation sounded a lot like the plot of an old monster movie where a doctor built a creature out of spare body parts and brought it to life. *Like Frankenstein*, she thought.

The creature groaned and cried some more. It was deep and loud, making the metal dumpster vibrate.

"Is it dangerous?" Flo asked.

"I'm not sure," Furry said. "But you saw what it did to the building. I think it's safe to say it might be dangerous."

"But it's crying," Flo said. She felt bad for the big guy.

Without warning, the golem lifted its head and turned to look straight at Furry and Flo. The creature had a giant face with a flat nose and two bright green glowing eyes. Its mouth was partially opened, and Flo saw a few blunt teeth carved inside.

Better than the sharp fangs of a vampire, she thought.

"WHY YOU WATCH ME," the golem said, its voice deep and booming. "LEAVE GARVEL BE."

Flo stepped forward, keeping her lunchbox close to her leg. It wouldn't do much good if the golem attacked, but it made her feel safer.

"What're you doing?" Furry whispered.

Flo ignored him, focusing her attention on the creature in front of her. "I'm Flo," she said, looking into the giant's green eyes. "What did you say your name was? Gravel?"

"GARVEL," the golem said.

"Maybe you *should* change it to Gravel," Furry muttered. "That makes more sense."

Flo shot her friend a look. "Furry!"

"I'm just saying . . ."

"MY NAME GARVEL," Garvel insisted. He edged himself off the dumpster and came down on his massive feet, shaking the ground beneath him. Standing up, the golem towered over Flo by at least ten feet.

How did he ever get out here? Flo wondered. She realized the golem must've squeezed through the holes he made in the apartment building and garage door.

"Nice to meet you, Garvel," Flo said. "You're not here to hurt us, are you?"

"MASTER SENT ME," Garvel said. Flo saw bits of rock falling from his mouth as he spoke. "TO FIND WOLF SON."

"Uh-oh. Don't tell him, Flo!" Furry hissed.

Well, duh, Flo thought.

"I NOT HURT FO," Garvel said. "I JUST WANT BROTHERS AND SISTERS BACK."

"Brothers and sisters back?" Flo said. "Your brothers and sisters?" She turned to Furry, who just shrugged in confusion.

"MASTER PROMISED. PULLED PIN," Garvel grumbled. "NOW THEY LOST AND APART."

Almost instantly, Garvel started weeping again. He put a hand to his face. It was odd behavior, considering Flo didn't see any tears.

"Pin?" Flo was beyond confused.

Furry stepped forward, still a bit hesitant. "I think I know what he's talking about," he whispered. "When a golem is created, the master puts a magic pin somewhere on it. When you pull it out, the magic that gives them life disappears. The golem just stops moving."

Flo looked at Garvel. She couldn't help but feel bad for him.

"Sounds like his creator pulled the pin on his brothers and sisters," Furry said. "That's why he's crying. Or . . . sort of crying anyway."

"That's awful," Flo said.

"Yeah," Furry agreed sadly. "Poor guy."

Flo watched the golem and felt her heart break a bit. Based on what Garvel had said, she figured his master must have promised to reunite him with his golem family if he succeeded. It didn't seem like Garvel would hurt them. At least as long as he didn't realize that Furry was the "Wolf Son" he'd been sent to find.

"We could probably pull his pin out and be done with it —" Furry started to say.

"Furry!" Flo shouted, interrupting him.

"You didn't let me finish!" Furry protested. "That would be the easy way. But the easy way isn't always the right way."

"No," Flo said. "It's not." She watched the giant rock monster wipe away tears that didn't exist with his arm.

"He can't just run loose here, though," Furry said. "Look what he did to our building. Besides, it won't be long until . . ."

Furry suddenly stopped talking. His head perked up as if he heard something.

"What?" Flo asked. "What is it?"

"Someone's coming!"

NUMBER
19

CHAPTER 4

Flo paced back and forth frantically. She didn't know what to do. They couldn't very well hide Garvel — the giant rock golem was as hidden as well he could be in the alley behind Corman Towers. But she didn't want to just leave him there either.

Furry ran through the wrecked garage door as Flo tried to come up with a plan. If they could get Garvel back inside, they could send

him back to his own world. But if what Garvel had said was true, his master might pull his pin and destroy him if he came home empty-handed. Just as he'd done to Garvel's brothers and sisters.

But keeping him here won't work either, Flo thought. *People would find out about the crack . . . and maybe even Furry's secret. We can't have that.*

"What the heck is taking him so long?" Flo muttered under her breath as she watched the door. In moments, Furry returned. He wasn't alone.

"Curtis!" Flo shouted. She'd never been so happy to see the retired caretaker. "Oh, thank goodness it's you!"

Curtis wasn't wearing his usual grubby terrycloth robe. Instead he wore a pair of wrinkled khakis and a faded T-shirt. But despite his normal, if messy, clothing, Curtis still wore his slippers.

"Well, would you look at this fella?" Curtis said. He adjusted his thick glasses for a better look.

"I don't know what to do with him," Flo said. "He can't stay here —"

"I can see that," Curtis interrupted. "He's already wrecked enough here, thank you very much. There are people on their way here to survey the damage to the base —"

"WHERE IS WOLF SON?" Garvel asked, startling the three of them.

Furry kept his mouth shut, and Flo stepped forward.

"Garvel, we don't know who Wolf Son is," Flo said. She felt bad for lying, but she had no choice. "We need to hide you before there's trouble."

"NEED TO FIND WOLF SON," Garvel said. Bits of rock sifted through his teeth as he spoke. "BRING WOLF SON BACK, AND MASTER WILL BRING GARVEL TO BROTHERS AND SISTERS."

Flo suddenly had an idea. "What if we help you find your brothers and sisters?" she asked.

"YOU HELP ME, FO?" Garvel asked.

"What are you doing, Flo?" Furry hissed.

"Trying to come up with a solution," Flo hissed back. "Maybe we can sneak him back into the laundry room and help him somehow."

"How are we going to help him if his brothers and sisters are all back in my world?" Furry said. Suddenly, a lightbulb seemed to come on in his head. "Wait a minute . . . you're not talking about going back there, are you?"

"Yes . . . no," Flo said, before throwing her hands up in frustration. "I don't know! I just know we have to do something! We can't just send him back to his doom."

Furry shook his head. "I don't know about this."

"Where's your portal shard?" Flo asked, realizing the faded blue stone Furry normally wore on a cord around his neck was missing.

"I left it in my room," Furry replied. "After that mummy managed to grab it off my neck, I thought it might be safer that way."

"Well, go get it," Flo told him. "Just in case."

Furry sighed, then dashed back into the apartment building, leaving Curtis and Flo alone in the alleyway with Garvel.

"Garvel," Flo asked. "If we take your pin out, what happens?"

"GARVEL FALL APART," the golem replied, sounding distressed.

"Can you be put back together?" Flo asked. "Will the pin still work?"

"YES," Garvel said. "PIN HOLD MAGIC. PIN HOLD IT FOREVER."

Flo was quiet for a few minutes as she thought about the possibilities. She needed to figure out a way to get Garvel back inside before anyone saw him. Taking him apart seemed like the best way to do that — if he would let her.

"Will you let me pull it out?" Flo asked. "Just for a little bit. I'll put it back in."

"GARVEL AFRAID," the golem said. "TRUST FO?"

"Yes, Garvel. You can trust me," Flo said. "I promise."

Garvel gave a small, jerky nod and touched the back of his head with a giant finger. "HERE IS PIN," he said.

"Okay, Garvel," Flo said, smacking the side of the big metal dumpster with her hand. "I need you to climb inside here."

With Curtis's help, they heaved the lid open. There were only a few garbage bags inside. The trash service came on Saturdays, so the dumpster was mostly empty.

The golem did as Flo had asked. The dumpster's wheels squeaked beneath his weight as he climbed inside. Flo prayed the thing would hold — her plan depended on it.

"This portal is becoming a bigger problem all the time," Curtis muttered, running a hand through his wild white hair as he took in the sight before him.

Flo handed the former caretaker her lunchbox and tried climbing into the dumpster with Garvel. When she struggled, the golem reached down to gently pick her up and set her on top of his massive rock shoulders.

"Thanks," Flo said. She studied the back of Garvel's head, searching for something that looked like a magic pin, and discovered a number carved into the back of the golem's head. "19?" she said aloud.

"YES. I AM YOUNGEST BROTHER," Garvel announced.

"Hurry up, kid!" Curtis called up to her. He kept a nervous eye on the empty doorway. "The insurance inspectors are on their way

here to look at the damage this thing caused. And I don't know about you, but I don't want to have to explain how he got here."

Flo nodded, then found what she was looking for. Just beneath the carved numbers and between Garvel's shoulder blades, she saw a round metal ball attached to a peg. It almost looked like a doorknob. Flo touched it with her finger and felt the metal vibrate beneath her hand. "This has to be it," she whispered.

Flo wrapped her fingers around the metal sphere and pulled. The pin slid out easily, and instantly, Garvel went limp. The golem wobbled and fell apart, all of his pieces tumbling neatly into the dumpster. Flo landed on top of the golem pieces, a little rougher than she'd liked.

Seconds later, Furry zipped out of the mangled garage door, clutching his portal shard tightly in his hand. "Hey!" he exclaimed, looking at the pile of rubble. "What'd you do?"

RUBBLE SMUGGLE

CHAPTER 5

Moving the dumpster into the garage was a lot harder than Flo had anticipated. It helped when Furry tore down the rest of the garage door to make a clear path, but it was still exhausting. Even in pieces, Garvel was heavy.

"My back hurts just watching you," Curtis said as Furry grunted and pushed the dumpster in through the opening.

Flo helped guide the big metal box through the garage.

"Careful not to scratch my truck!" Curtis hollered at them.

Once inside, they spotted a few men with notebooks in the basement hallway. They seemed to be taking notes on the damage.

"This isn't good," Flo whispered. She opened her lunchbox and put Garvel's pin inside for safekeeping. It was a tight fit, but she managed to mash a sandwich or two to make room.

"Leave it to me," Curtis said. "I'll take them outside. You two get that rocky fella back where he belongs!"

Furry and Flo pushed the dumpster against the wall of the garage and hid nearby as Curtis approached the insurance adjusters. After a few minutes of chatting and motioning with his arms, Curtis guided the men to the other parts of the building that had sustained golem damage.

When the coast was clear, Furry and Flo wheeled the dumpster as close to the laundry room as they could manage. By the time they got there, Furry was panting like a thirsty dog.

"Man, even with my werewolf strength, this guy is heavy," Furry whispered.

Flo nodded in agreement. She was just glad Furry didn't have to change into his true form to use his strength. A golem would be hard enough to explain. But a werewolf too? Forget it.

"We have to hurry," Flo said. "Curtis can't keep those insurance guys out there forever."

Furry reached into the dumpster and lifted out a big chunk of Garvel. "Is this part of his arm?" he asked.

Flo studied the stony chunk. "I'm not sure," she admitted. With everything jumbled together in the dumpster, it was almost impossible to tell which pieces went where.

Flo carried a few of the lighter-weight golem pieces to the space behind the dryer. The blue portal crack was glowing brightly, almost as if it sensed the portal shard was near.

Furry hefted the rest of the golem into the laundry room as quickly as he could. Then they stood in their mostly hidden spot, staring at the pieces of Garvel.

"Can we even put him back together?" Furry said, picking up a chunk of stone. "This might be part of his leg."

Flo realized that her plan was falling apart — even faster than Garvel had. It was like looking at the world's heaviest, most complicated puzzle. She had no clue where to start.

Furry suddenly perked up as if he'd heard something, and he dropped the golem piece he'd been holding. It fell right into the portal crack and disappeared with a loud *WHOOSH!*

"Furry!" Flo cried.

"Sorry!" Furry whispered. "But someone's coming!"

By then Flo could hear them too. Footsteps were quickly approaching the laundry room, and she peeked over the top of the dryers just in time to see Curtis stick his head in the doorway.

"Time's up, kids!" Curtis hissed. "They're coming back here to examine the damage to the dryers!"

There's only one choice, Flo thought. She turned to Furry. "Quick, knock the rest of him in!"

Before Furry could say anything, Flo started shoving every piece she could move into the crack. *WHOOSH, WHOOSH, WHOOSH!*

"What're we doing?" Furry exclaimed, heaving piece after piece into the portal. "Are we leaving him in pieces over there?"

"No," Flo said as Garvel's last part *WHOOSHED* back to the monster world. "We're going in after him!"

Before Furry could protest, she grabbed him, held onto her lunchbox, and jumped into the crack.

WHOOSH!

* * *

Flo knew she'd never get used to jumping through the portal. She'd only done it twice before — once while chasing a troublesome mummy back to Furry's world and then again on the trip back home. Flying through the portal felt like riding the fastest part of a roller coaster. The air whipped past Flo's face, and she felt like she was flying a million miles an hour.

And just like that, it stopped.

Flo suddenly found herself facedown on a flat piece of mossy stone. The air was thin and cool and smelled like a forest. In the distance, Flo saw huge hunks of rock, all seemingly floating through a blue sky filled with clouds. They looked like sky islands, and they were everywhere. It looked nothing like what she remembered of Furry's world.

"Ouch," Furry groaned next to her. He had landed on top of the biggest chunk of Garvel and was already in his werewolf form. As Furry had explained during their first trip back to his world, he was *always* a werewolf in his world. He didn't have a choice one way or the other.

"I hope Curtis covered the portal," Flo said, sitting up. "Otherwise, those insurance guys are definitely going to find it."

Furry leapt to his feet, standing on top of the gravel that used to be Garvel. "He won't need to, remember?" he said, holding his portal shard. "When this comes back with me, the portal closes."

Flo got to her feet and looked at the small stone circle they'd passed through. There was only a sliver of the crack open, and in seconds, it was sealed tight. The passage back to her world was closed.

"Same deal as before," Furry said, sifting through the pieces of the broken golem. "Once the sun sets here, the portal shifts, and it won't lead back to Corman Towers again."

Flo nodded. "Got it," she said. "Let's get him put back together quickly then."

"There's just one problem," Furry said. "If we get him put back together, it's going to be pretty obvious that I'm the Wolf Son he was sent to find."

"We told him we'd help him," Flo said. "Let's just hope that's enough and that he really only cares about finding his little golem family."

Furry laughed. "*Little* family," he said. "That's hilarious."

Flo opened her lunchbox and pulled the large pin out. It was still warm, and she felt it vibrate. "This goes between his shoulders," Flo said, tossing it to her friend.

Furry caught it in his hairy paws. "Okay," he said. "Where's his head?"

Flo scanned the mossy expanse, looking off to where the horizon seemed to disappear. She saw it and groaned. "It's rolling down the hill!"

THE HILLS
ARE
ALIVE

CHAPTER 6

Flo took off running as fast as she could. Her tennis shoes pounded on the mossy stone, and her legs knocked taller grasses aside. Thankfully the hill was a gradual slope, so Garvel's head hadn't gotten very far. It was only about twenty yards away, but it was picking up speed.

"Flo!" Furry cried. "Wait!"

"Keep building him!" Flo shouted over her shoulder. "I got this!"

As the head rolled on, Flo picked up speed. She was worried that every second they kept Garvel in pieces hurt their chances of bringing him back to life. Stopping the head would be the easy part. Putting him back together would require the heavy lifting. *Werewolf work*, she thought.

When she was a few feet away, Flo heard something that nearly stopped her in her tracks — small growls and rustling coming from the tall grass.

Suddenly the grasses parted, and small, fanged beasts leapt out. A fuzzy little creature with bulbous eyes and fangs snapped at Flo's heels. Flo screamed and deftly swatted it away with her Dyno-Katz lunchbox. It tumbled to the ground with a whimper, but righted itself again. Another lunged at her foot, but Flo

kicked it, watching it roll away like a hairy
soccer ball.

Glancing behind her, Flo was amazed to
see that Furry had all but finished building
Garvel. The only thing missing was his head.

"Should I put the pin in?" Furry shouted.

Flo had no way of knowing if Garvel would
be brought to life if he wasn't fully assembled,

but she figured it couldn't hurt to try. "Yes!" she shouted.

Furry pushed the pin into the headless golem. Flo turned just in time to see Garvel's eyes light up in his still-rolling stone head.

"Whoa," Flo said. She was within four feet of the head, but it was rolling faster now. Up ahead, the land just . . . disappeared. Flo knew if she didn't stop it, Garvel's head would roll right off the edge.

"HI, FO," Garvel's voice boomed as his face rolled over again.

"Hi, Garvel," Flo said. "We're in a bit of trouble."

"GARVEL SEES," the golem said with no emotion. "HERE I COME."

Just then, Flo heard thundering footsteps approaching from behind her. She glanced over her shoulder and saw Furry running toward her. The headless golem was right on his heels.

"He's after me, Flo!" Furry cried. The little werewolf was clearly terrified.

"No, he's not — he's after his head!" Flo shouted, still dodging little monsters and chasing after the golem's head. In another twenty yards, the head would be lost forever. One of the little beasts nipped at her leg, tearing a hole in her sock. It stung like nobody's business.

Realizing she was nearly out of space, Flo dove, reaching out for Garvel's head. She caught the face by the nose, managing to stop it just a few feet from the edge.

The fall knocked the wind right out of her. Breathless, Flo turned around to see Furry swiping at the little monsters with his paws. They were everywhere now, swarming from all sides.

"TURN MY HEAD, FO. SEE HILLTOOTHS," Garvel said.

Flo wasn't sure how his head worked while disconnected from the body, but she obeyed. She turned Garvel's head so that his glowing green eyes saw Furry, the hillside, and all the little monsters attacking them.

"THANK YOU," Garvel said. His headless body suddenly leaped into the air, coming down mere feet from Furry. The impact of his heavy feet hitting the ground was tremendous. The little monsters Garvel had called hilltooths went airborne. As they flew into the air, the golem swung his big stony fists. He knocked half a dozen one direction and sent another five sailing clear off the edge of the floating landmass.

Next the headless golem raised his fist, crashing it down on the ground. The blow

smashed a few more hilltooths, and Garvel kicked the remaining handful away from Furry.

"Is he going to get me?" Furry asked. He bounded toward Flo, acting like a dog with his tail between his legs. "Does he know who I am?"

"I NO HURT YOU, WOLF SON," Garvel said. "YOU HELP GARVEL."

"Cool," the little werewolf said with a nod. "I'm Furry."

"FERDY," Garvel repeated.

"Close enough," Furry replied.

The rest of the hilltooths darted away, retreating to their little holes in the floating stone. Satisfied, Garvel's headless body brushed the mashed monster bits from his hands and stomped over to Furry and Flo.

Then the golem reached down, picked up his head, and set it back on his body where it belonged.

"Better?" Flo asked.

"BETTER," Garvel said with a relieved, rocky sigh.

Flo got to her feet and brushed mashed moss from her legs. "So," she said, "this is your home. Nice."

Flo looked around the floating rock. It was like something out of a movie. The floating landmasses were everywhere. There almost seemed to be more chunks of stone and greenery drifting by than clouds.

"YES," Garvel said. "FLOAT ROCK. MASTER LIVE HERE TOO."

As Flo eyed the sky, three feathered things that resembled snakes zigzagged across the sky. Off in the trees, something croaked like an oversized frog.

"Have you been here before, Furry?" Flo asked. "This place is beautiful. A bit dangerous, but beautiful."

"No," Furry admitted. "I've heard of Float Rock Canyon, though. I think that's where we are. It's far from where I used to live, but I heard some of the grownups talk about the giants living up in the sky. This must be it. I never realized the giants were actually golems created by magic."

Flo turned and looked up at Garvel. "Let's speak to your master," she said. "We need to find out where your brothers and sisters are."

Garvel turned his head, making Flo cringe at the sound of stone scraping together. Little bits of dust sifted down his large body. The golem looked uphill and pointed. "THROUGH TREES," Garvel said flatly. "HE WILL BE ANGRY WITH GARVEL."

Flo frowned. "Well, that's nothing compared to how angry I am with him," she said. "Let's go."

Flo set off up the hill, walking toward the towering trees. When the others didn't immediately follow her, she turned. "I said, let's go, boys."

NOT A
NICE GUY

CHAPTER 7

The floating chunk of land they were on seemed much larger than the others drifting through the sky. Flo felt her legs grow tired the higher they climbed. She didn't care, though. She wanted to find the golem master and give him a piece of her mind.

"Do think this is a good idea, Flo?" Furry asked, walking beside her on all fours. He still eyed Garvel carefully, as if unsure he could trust him. "When his master sees me, won't he think Garvel captured me? After all, that's why he was sent."

Flo froze and grabbed the little werewolf's hairy shoulders. "Furry, you're a genius!" she exclaimed. "That's exactly what we should do. We pretend Garvel has captured you. He brings you to his master, and we uncover where the rest of the golems are. It's perfect!"

It's going to be a golem family reunion, Flo thought happily. She just hoped the other golems were as great as Garvel.

But Furry didn't share her enthusiasm. "I don't like it," he said, shaking his head.

"Come on, think about it," Flo said, trying to keep up with Garvel and convince Furry at the same time.

Up ahead, the golem stepped on a fallen tree that was almost as thick as a subway tunnel. The tree was mashed flat, making it easier for Furry and Flo to follow him. As they continued climbing the stony terrain, Flo spotted hilltooths in the grass, watching. None of them seemed brave enough to come out, though. Not with Garvel around.

"What's to think about?" Furry said. "He's leading us straight to the guy who wanted to capture me and bring me back."

"Yeah, but Garvel won't turn on us," Flo insisted. "We helped him, remember?"

"You don't know that for sure," Furry said. "His master might get control of him again."

Flo didn't think that would happen — or at least she hoped it wouldn't. It seemed like Garvel acted on his own.

Up ahead, Flo noticed an off-kilter sign nailed to one of the trees. On it were a series of markings that Flo couldn't read. "Can you read that?" she asked Furry, pointing to the sign.

"Yeah," Furry said. "It says, 'Turn In Fear! Those Who Would Dare Enter Here.'"

Flo shook her head. "'Keep Out' would've worked just as well," she said.

It was a joke, but Furry wasn't laughing. Flo knew his senses were on full alert. Every rustle in the grass and smell that drifted through the chilly air caught his attention.

"We're going to be fine," Flo whispered.

"I hope you're right," Furry replied, glancing over his shoulder. The portal they'd come through was a long way away. "Let's just help him find those golem guys and get back home."

* * *

After almost twenty minutes of walking, the golem stopped. "WE HERE, FERDY AND FO," Garvel said.

It wasn't exactly clear where here was. They stood before a tall crudely built stone wall. A large iron gate appeared to be the only way inside.

Flo cautiously stepped forward and approached the gate. She peered through the narrow openings between the slender metal bars. Up ahead was a small run-down-looking cottage. Next to that stood a large work area covered with a metal roof, rusted and warped with age.

Beneath the ramshackle roof, Flo could see a variety of tools hanging from freestanding wooden racks. A massive dark shape was situated in the middle of the ground, but from where Flo stood she couldn't tell what it was.

Just then, a man wearing a filthy apron appeared. His head was bald, save for a thin

ring of white around the outside edge. The man walked over to a nearby workbench and tapped something, making a loud clanging noise.

Furry squeezed in next to Flo and pointed. "That has to be Garvel's master," he whispered.

"Not for long," Flo whispered back.

The rotund man, who was as short as he was wide, suddenly turned to face the gate. He glared in their direction, and his forehead wrinkled as if he'd spent his whole life frowning. The man waddled a few steps toward the gate and shouted, "You've brought him to me! The Wolf Son!"

Garvel leaned over them and shoved the gate open. It groaned and creaked on rusty hinges. The nearby wall section wobbled a bit, looking as though a flick of Garvel's finger could topple it.

"Last chance, Flo," Furry said. "If we go now, we can make it back to the portal and get out of here."

Flo shook her head. "We have to help Garvel," she said. "I promised. Besides, if we escape, who knows what his master will do?"

Furry sighed, and the two friends slowly made their way inside the gate.

The golem master's face broke into a crooked grin as they approached, making him look even more unpleasant. "And who else have you brought?" he asked. "An other-worlder? Some girl? What good is she going to do me?"

Rude much? Flo thought. She felt her anger rise to the surface and clutched her

lunchbox tightly to try to keep herself under control. As the man came even closer, Flo noticed something jangling on the leather belt around his work apron.

A cluster of golem pins.

The hearts of all of Garvel's brothers and sisters, Flo thought. *His master has them —*

which means all those golems are lifeless somewhere.

Flo took a brave step forward. "We're here for Garvel's brothers and sisters," she called.

"His brothers and sisters," the man repeated with a mean laugh. "Those golems are my creations and not your concern."

"You can't just give life to something and then take it away!" Flo shouted. She felt brave with a werewolf and a golem on her side.

"I will do as I wish!" the golem master yelled at her. "I am Krigg of the Upper Lands! Who do you think you are, other-worlder, speaking to me like this?"

The golem master glared at Flo, and Flo glared right back. His mouth cracked open in a sneer, and Flo saw his strange little round teeth were like white pushpins. "You should not have come here, other-worlder," he said. "Number 19! I command you to grab the Wolf Son!"

"No!" Flo shouted. Garvel turned toward them, and Furry crouched down, ready to spring into action.

"And toss this girl into Float Rock Canyon!" Krigg shouted.

TWENTY
IS PLENTY

CHAPTER 8

Furry turned on all fours and took off running toward the gate. As he did, it swung shut, locking them inside the walled area.

"There will be no escape," Krigg said. He raised his hammer over his head in triumph. "The reward for your capture is mine, Wolf Son!"

"What reward? Who hired you to find me?" Furry shouted as he scanned the top of the wall. Flo knew Furry could easily jump over the top and escape to the other side. But she also knew Furry would never leave her in danger.

"Nobody hired me!" Krigg shouted. "Everyone knows what you did and the riches they'll receive for bringing you in!"

The golem thundered toward Flo. With every step he took, the ground shook.

"Garvel, no," Flo pleaded. She looked into Garvel's glowing green eyes, hoping to see some reaction, but there was no emotion on his face. He was coming for her and Furry, and there was nothing either of them could do.

Furry was right, Flo thought. *This was a dumb idea.*

Garvel towered above Flo and stopped. He glanced down at her, then turned to face Krigg, who was watching with a smirk on his face.

"NO HURT FO," Garvel said. "NO CAPTURE WOLF SON."

Krigg's smirk immediately disappeared. "What?" he shouted. He dropped his hammer, just missing his own boot, and his face turned red with anger. "I am your master! You will do as I command, Number 19!"

"I WILL NOT," Garvel replied.

"Then you will be destroyed like the eighteen failures that came before you!" Krigg cried.

The golem master turned and ran toward his outdoor workshop. Flo saw him fumble with something on his belt. Garvel took a cautious step toward Krigg and his cottage.

"Flo, c'mon!" Furry shouted frantically from his position near the gate. "I can get us out of here!"

But Flo couldn't move. She watched Krigg pull a pin from his belt and jam it into the dark mass on the ground. The bulky figure uncurled itself, revealing a massive body. It stood up on its enormous legs, knocking the roof off the workshop in the process. The giant stepped forward, and the light from the sun glinted off its metallic body.

"An iron golem," Flo whispered.

The metal giant stood at attention in front of the ruined workshop. Krigg, his wicked smile back in place, proudly looked up at the massive monster. The iron golem was fashioned from giant plates of metal, which had been made to look like medieval armor. His head was a helmet but instead of two green eyes, like Garvel had, the iron golem's eyes glowed red.

"Number 20!" Krigg shouted. "Destroy these trespassers, and bring the Wolf Son to me!"

"YES, MASTER," the iron golem replied. Without another word, he turned and ran toward them.

Garvel turned to Flo. "HIDE, FO," he said.

Flo turned and ran toward the wall where Furry still stood.

"Are we ready to get out of here yet?" Furry cried. He held his arms out like a cradle, motioning for Flo to hop in. But she didn't. Instead, she turned and watched from the closed gate.

Number 20 swung his massive iron fist, catching Garvel across his chiseled face. The stone golem staggered, and chunks of rock fell from his chin. Garvel's footsteps boomed as he tried to find his balance.

Number 20 followed up with a kick, driving his rivet-covered boot into Garvel's torso. In moments, the rock golem was falling. The massive floating chunk of rock they stood on shook as his body hit the ground.

"He never had a chance," Flo whispered. She watched in horror as the iron golem stepped forward, grabbed Garvel's right arm, and tugged.

"No!" Flo cried.

"I AM BROTHER," Garvel said in his flat, stony voice.

"YOU MUST BE DESTROYED," Number 20 said. "AS COMMANDED."

With another mighty tug, Garvel's right arm came loose. The iron golem looked at it, then down at Garvel. He dropped the stone arm and lifted his foot, bringing it crashing down on Garvel's torso.

"No!" Flo screamed. She raced to the now-motionless rock golem. Number 20 turned in her direction as if ready to fight his next target.

"Flo, are you crazy?" Furry shouted. He ran after his friend and caught her shirt in his teeth, pulling her to a stop. "We can't fight this thing! There's nothing we can do!"

"We have to see if Garvel is okay!" Flo cried, feeling the tears well up in her eyes. "He's not moving!"

"DESTROY TRESPASSER," Number 20 rumbled. His voice vibrated through the floating lands. "RETRIEVE WOLF SON."

"Stop!" Flo shouted. She raised her lunchbox up as if prepared to strike. "Don't do this! You're not a monster! You don't have to do what he says!"

Number 20 raised his iron fist in the air and brought it down inches from where Furry and Flo stood. The impact shook the ground, knocking them both off their feet. Flo's lunchbox clattered away and popped open, spilling sandwiches, chips, and juice pouches across the ground.

Furry leapt to his feet and stood in front of Flo as Number 20 raised his fist again. "If you squash her, you'll have to squash me too!" the little werewolf shouted.

But before the iron golem could do anything, a rocky hand grasped his shoulder. Garvel stood behind his younger, stronger brother and pulled him away. "NO HURT FO AND FURDY," the golem said in his usual, flat tone.

Garvel gave the iron golem a push backward, and Number 20 tripped over his own legs. He fell against the far wall, smashing a giant hole in the rocky border. Garvel moved to help his brother up, but when he saw through the hole in the wall, he stopped in his tracks. Number 20 turned to look too.

"Stop!" Krigg shouted, running toward his creations. "Get away! I told you! Never look over that wall! I command you both to come away from there!"

Furry helped Flo to her feet. She watched the golems in confusion. Only moments before, they'd seemed intent on destroying each other. But now they seemed completely distracted by something else.

GRAVEYARD

CHAPTER 9

Flo ran to the golems standing near the destroyed section of the rock wall. As she approached, Krigg continued to rant at his creations.

"Move away from there!" he shouted. "I command you! Now!"

Flo stepped beneath Garvel's legs and climbed over a toppled part of the wall. Furry was right on her tail. He handed her the Dyno-Katz lunchbox she'd had knocked from her hand.

"Thanks," Flo said gratefully.

"No problem," Furry replied.

They both turned to see what had the golem brothers' attention, and when Flo saw what lay on the other side of the wall, she gasped.

Just outside the barrier, spread among the long grasses, were golem parts. Heads, arms, legs, feet. They were everywhere. Some of the golems were partially put together, while others were completely disassembled. A smaller golem, which looked to be made of wood, leaned against a rock. Its dark, empty eyes stared at the ground, as if too sad to see what had happened to the others.

"It's a golem graveyard," Flo whispered. Deemed failures, they'd been tossed aside as Krigg began work on his next version.

"BROTHERS," Garvel said. "SISTERS."

The rock golem reached down with his remaining arm and helped Number 20 to his feet. The iron golem stood up next to his older brother. Neither of them said anything as they took in the scene in front of them.

"Number 20!" Krigg shouted, just yards behind them. "You will not defy me! I am your master! You will destroy these intruders! Do as I command, or I will pull the life from you!"

Flo spun around furiously. "You will not!" she shouted, her temperature rising. "You will not build another one of these creatures only to toss them away like garbage!"

"I grow tired of —" Krigg began.

"Number 20!" Flo interrupted. "Retrieve the pins from Krigg. We're bringing your family back together!"

Without hesitation, Number 20 turned away from his older brother and the rest of his dismantled siblings. He took a thundering step toward Krigg, who stood with his mouth open in shock.

"I'd drop the pins if I were you," Flo told him.

"Yeah," Furry agreed. "Don't be dumb, Krigg."

Krigg fumbled with the belt cinched around his apron as Number 20 took another step toward him. The rock pile beneath Flo's feet trembled.

"No, no!" Krigg cried. "This isn't right! I command you, not her!"

"Doesn't look that way," Flo said. "Now that he knows what you've done, you're not in charge anymore."

Krigg freed the belt and slipped the ring of pins from it. He held it out, his hand trembling in fear.

"DROP THEM," Number 20 commanded. "RUN FAR FROM HERE."

Krigg didn't need to be told twice. He immediately surrendered the pins and took off running as fast as his stubby legs could carry him. He raced through the iron gate and headed for the hills.

"And never come back!" Flo shouted after him. As she watched him run, she couldn't help but think, *I hope the hilltooths are hungry.*

Furry jumped down from the toppled wall and ran over to where the cluster of metal pins lay on the ground. Picking them up in his mouth, he carried them over to Flo.

Flo took the pins, wiped off the werewolf slobber, and looked through the collection. Each pin had a number carved onto the surface of the pinhead — probably corresponding to the golem it brought to life.

Behind her, Flo heard Garvel's heavy footsteps. Both she and Furry turned to see the golem walking among the remains of his brothers and sisters. It was heartbreaking to see the silent golem look at what was left of his family.

A moment later, Number 20 returned with Garvel's arm. He walked over, turned to his older brother, and reattached the chunk of rock to his shoulder.

Garvel moved his arm as if to get the feel for it again. "BROTHER," he said.

"BROTHER," Number 20 said in agreement.

"We should put everyone back together,"
Flo said to Furry, holding up the ring of pins.

"Sure," Furry said. "I like that idea."

They climbed down into the golem graveyard to help sort out the pieces. As Flo wandered among the silent heads of Garvel's family, she couldn't help but feel a bit creeped out. She tried to imagine what might have angered Krigg so much that he'd decided to take them apart and toss them aside.

As they walked, it became clear that nearly all the golems were made of different material. One was made of dirt, another of clay. Nearby lay a golem head made of something Flo was afraid might be bone. "Gross," she muttered. She didn't even want to *think* about where Krigg found the materials to build *that* one.

Furry, Flo, and the golems worked together, moving matching pieces close to the bodies they belonged to. Number 20 and Garvel did the heavy work. They set heads atop necks and torsos and attached arms and legs to rebuild their odd family.

As each golem was completed, Flo found the corresponding pin and gave it to Garvel.

"THANK YOU, FO," Garvel said each time. The golem was polite. Flo liked that.

One by one, Garvel pressed the magic metal into the bodies of his brothers and sisters. As they were reactivated, the first thing the golems saw was their younger sibling welcoming them back with his rocky face and gentle green eyes.

"YOU ARE HOME," Garvel said to them. And if any of the golems could've smiled, Flo imagined they would have.

GOLEM GORGE

CHAPTER 10

Furry and Flo worked late into the afternoon, arranging pieces and watching the revived golems bring the others back to life.

The reanimated golems seemed lost at first, making Flo wonder how long they'd been dismantled. Number 1, a golem made from a salt-like substance, was also the smallest. He looked as though he'd been left in the field for some time. Parts of his face had eroded, and he was cracked in places.

"Do you think Krigg will come back?" Furry asked, watching the giants move around. They seemed unsure what to do with themselves.

"I don't think so," Flo said. "There are twenty of these guys, and he couldn't even get his newest one to obey him."

Furry watched the golems. "I don't know how anyone could throw these guys away."

Flo brushed her hair from her eyes. There was a lot she didn't understand. "Krigg made it sound like everyone is trying to bring you back," she said. "Do you think that's really true?"

Furry shrugged and fished the portal shard from his shorts pocket. He held it in his hairy hand. "It's this thing," he said. "It being gone leaves this place exposed. Just like it opens up your world to stuff coming over from mine."

Flo watched Garvel bring back a golem that looked as if it was made from dead trees and vines. The giant stretched, and Flo swore she heard the sound of creaking wood.

"I don't understand how *anything* from your world would be afraid of anything from mine," Flo said. "You have golems, goblins, skeletons, vampires . . ."

"Werewolves," Furry added, playfully elbowing Flo in the ribs. "But not all of us are scary, right? I'm a pretty nice guy."

"Yeah," Flo said with a smile. "Sorta."

Just then, Garvel approached them. "FO," he said. "SISTER THREE HAS NO PIN."

Flo glanced at the empty pin ring in Garvel's hand, then over to where a crystal golem was assembled out on the ground. "Okay, Garvel," Flo said. "We'll go look."

Furry ran over to the crystal golem to get a noseful. Once he had the scent, he nodded toward Krigg's cottage. "It might be in there," he said. "Should we look?"

"Yeah," Flo said. She only hoped Number 3's pin wasn't lost for good.

* * *

Furry and Flo approached the small worn cottage cautiously. Flo knew that Krigg was likely long gone, but she still wanted to be careful.

"Do you smell anything?" she asked Furry.

Furry kept his nose to the ground and approached the front door of Krigg's cottage on all fours. Finally he looked up. "It's in there," he said. "And close by."

Flo cautiously opened the door, which groaned on squeaky hinges. Inside was a crude kitchen that seemed to double as a laboratory. There were papers and drawings everywhere. Tools were scattered next to uneaten food, and large books were opened to pages filled with writing Flo couldn't read.

Furry slipped inside. He caught a whiff of something and sneezed four rapid-fire times.

"Jeez! Are you okay?" Flo asked, stepping into the cottage.

"Yeah." Furry sneezed again. "Dust."

Flo walked around the dimly lit room in amazement. It was such a mess, she had no idea how Krigg got anything done, let alone built a golem. As she glanced at the stacks of illegible books and journals, she paused.

From the other side of the room, Furry let out an excited yip. "Hey, I found it," he cried.

"I found something too," Flo said, picking up a piece of stiff parchment paper.

Flo looked over to see Furry trying to pull a crystal pin from a piece of cord attached to the ceiling. *Krigg must have kept it separate from the metal ones to keep it from breaking*, she thought.

In moments, Furry tugged it free. "What did you find?" he asked.

Flo held up the parchment. On it were more words she couldn't read along with a drawing — of Furry.

"Oh," Furry said. "Look at that."

"Can you read it?" Flo asked.

Furry looked a little uncomfortable, but he nodded. He took the paper and with a small sigh said, "Rolvis of the High Pack of Were—"

"What's a Rolvis?" Flo asked.

"Not what — who. It's my dad," Furry said. "His name is Rolvis."

"Sorry," Flo said. "Go on."

"Let's see," Furry said, finding his place. "Oh, here we go. Rolvis seeks help in the recovery of his missing son, the werewolf . . ." His voice trailed off.

"What? Why did you stop?" Flo asked.

"I kind of don't want to tell you my real name," Furry said. "It's embarrassing."

"What do you mean?" Flo asked. "I know your real name — it's Ferdinand."

Furry shook his head. "That's the name Mona and Jorge gave me when Curtis brought me to them as a baby," he said. "But it's not my real name. Plus, I like being called Furry."

Flo shrugged. She hadn't realized Furry's name had come from his adoptive parents. *I guess there's a lot I still don't know*, she thought. "Okay," she said. "I guess you don't have to tell me."

"Someday, okay?" Furry said. "Anyway, the rest of this poster thing says my dad will pay a fortune in bellims to whoever manages to return his son — and the portal shard."

"Bellims?" Flo repeated.

"It's like money in my world," Furry explained.

"Jeez," Flo said. "You'd think he'd just be happy to have you back."

Furry shrugged. "That's my dad, I guess."

Flo looked outside. The sun was lower in the sky now, and they still had to trek back to the portal before the sun went down. "Let's get this back to Garvel so he can bring his last sister back to life," she said.

Furry took one last look at the poster before he crumpled it up and tossed it away.

Something tells me Furry is leaving some stuff out, Flo thought. It was hard when you knew that your best friend was keeping something from you — whether that something was good or bad.

THE PROBLEM WITH PORTALS

CHAPTER 11

Furry and Flo left the cottage and found the reanimated golems walking around the walled-in courtyard. Number 20 crouched down and held his hand out to them.

"Here you go," Furry said, gently placing the crystal pin into the iron golem's hand.

"THANK YOU, WOLF SON," Number 20 said. He walked back to the golem graveyard to revive the last of his siblings.

The rest of the golems were busy smashing the walls of their former prison. The crudely made wall came down in moments. Number 12, a golem made of a shiny black material, hurled the iron gate through the woods, clearing out their new home.

"Wow," Flo said. "These guys didn't waste any time."

"I wonder what they'll do with themselves now," Furry said. "They were so used to being bossed around."

"They'll think of something," Flo said. She looked up at the sky. The sun was still high enough that she wasn't too nervous, but she didn't want to waste too much time. She didn't want to think about what would happen if the portal shifted.

Just then Garvel caught sight of them. He immediately turned away from what he was working on and approached with heavy footsteps.

"Hi," Flo said, looking up at the stone golem. Of all the monsters that had found their way through the portal, Garvel was her favorite — other than Furry, of course.

"WHAT IS YOUR COMMAND?" Garvel asked.

"What?" Flo said, glancing at Furry. "I don't have any commands for you."

"Well," Furry said, "maybe one last command. More like a favor. Can a couple of you guys protect us as we head back home? From those hilltooth things?"

"YES, FURDY," Garvel said. He walked toward Number 6, a mud golem, and Number 11, who seemed to be made of plastic. The stone golem said something, pointed to Furry and Flo, and waved them over.

"Ready to go home?" Flo asked.

"Oh, yeah," Furry said as the two of them headed toward the space where the gate had once stood.

As they walked past, the golems all turned and looked at them, the two little strangers who had helped bring them back to life. Each of them gave a nod of appreciation.

"YOU ARE FRIENDS," Garvel said.

* * *

Their journey back to the portal was much easier. Flo looked around at the strange trees, which seemed larger than the ones back home. More snake-like birds twisted across the sky, and a creature she'd never heard before made some sort of shrill chirping noise.

Flo took a deep breath of fresh air. It was so much better than the air where she lived.

"It's really beautiful here," she said to no one in particular.

"Yeah," Furry said. "Some parts of my world are really pretty. I bet you thought it was all just mummies and haunted houses, huh?"

"Not exactly," Flo said. She remembered being shocked when they'd ended up in the desert during their previous trip to Furry's world. It wasn't what she'd imagined at all. And knowing that there were giant floating rocks hovering above the rest of Furry's world? The place definitely kept her guessing.

A hilltooth suddenly sprang out of the bushes just as Garvel stepped down — hard. The ground vibrated, and the little beast ran away with a yip. Flo looked up at the stone golem in appreciation. Garvel nodded to her.

"I wonder where Krigg ended up," Furry said, looking around. He sniffed the air a few times. "He came through this way. I can smell him. He probably can't get too far. I wonder how big this chunk of rock is."

"As long as he leaves the golems alone, he can go wherever he wants," Flo said.

As they neared the location of the portal, Furry's nose really perked up. The little werewolf got down on all fours and sniffed around frantically.

"What is it?" Flo asked. She watched as the golems around her stamped the high grasses, sending more hilltooths scattering.

"Krigg was just here," Furry said. "A few minutes ago."

"Can you tell where he is now?" Flo asked, looking around.

"I hear someone farther away from here. Sounds like a lot of snapping through bushes and shouting," Furry said. "Sounds like he might have his hands full with the hilltooths."

"Good," Flo said. "Serves him right."

A few yards from the portal stone, Flo saw something that made her heart skip a beat. Lying there in the trampled grass was a hammer — Krigg's hammer.

"He was here," Flo said. She ran over and picked up the hammer. The wooden handle was warm, as if someone had held it recently.

Furry groaned. "He sure was," he said. "Look what he did!"

Flo was afraid to look, but she joined Furry at the moss-covered stone. The portal was not as they had left it. It had been smashed repeatedly, leaving it a cracked, ruined mess.

Chunks of the stone were scattered nearby. Some had been crushed to powder.

"Krigg," Flo whispered. "Oh, no. What has he done?"

Furry growled and kicked a nearby stone down the hill in anger. "I'll tell you what he's done," he said. "He's trapped us here!"

Flo's eyes grew huge. "Wait! Can't we fix it? Maybe your shard will still work!"

Furry shook his head. He pulled the small shard from his pocket and tried to draw a line through the crumbled pieces. The shard couldn't even mark anything, let alone leave a line to reopen a crack.

"We're stuck," Furry said. He almost threw the shard in frustration but stopped himself. He instead threw back his head and howled into the blue sky.

"YOU GO HOME NOW?" Garvel said.

Flo sat down on the ground, stunned. She felt the eyes of hundreds of hilltooths watching her and thought, *What if this is our home now?*

THE AUTHOR

Thomas Kingsley Troupe has written more than thirty children's books. His book *Legend of the Werewolf* (Picture Window Books, 2011) received a bronze medal for the Moonbeam Children's Book Award. Thomas lives in Woodbury, Minnesota with his wife and two young boys.

THE ILLUSTRATOR

Stephen Gilpin is the illustrator of several dozen children's books and is currently working on a project he hopes will give him the ability to walk through walls — although he acknowledges there is still a lot of work to be done on this project. He currently lives in Hiawatha, Kansas, with his genius wife, Angie, and their kids.

CATCH UP
ON ALL SIX OF
FURRY
AND FLO'S
ADVENTURES